The Ghost Who Haunted the Capitol

by
Steve Brezenoff

illustrated by
C. B. Canga

STONE ARCH BOOKS
a capstone imprint

f Samantha Archer,

Field Trip Mysteries are published by Stone Arch Books
A Capstone Imprint
151 Good Counsel Drive, P.O. Box 669
Mankato, Minnesota 56002
www.capstonepub.com

Library of Congress Cataloging-in-Publication Data is
available on the Library of Congress website.

Library binding: 978-1-4342-2140-7
Paperback: 978-1-4342-2772-0

Art Director/Graphic Designer:
Kay Fraser

Summary:
In Washington, D.C. on a field trip, Edward
"Egg" Garrison and his friends solve a
haunting mystery.

Printed in the United States of America in Stevens Point,
Wisconsin.
032010
005741WZF10

TABLE OF CONTENTS

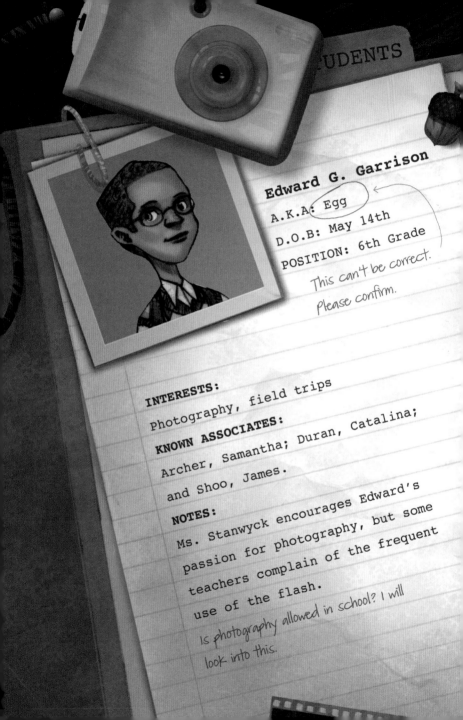

Edward G. Garrison

A.K.A: Egg

D.O.B: May 14th

POSITION: 6th Grade

This can't be correct.
Please confirm.

INTERESTS:

Photography, field trips

KNOWN ASSOCIATES:

Archer, Samantha; Duran, Catalina;
and Shoo, James.

NOTES:

Ms. Stanwyck encourages Edward's
passion for photography, but some
teachers complain of the frequent
use of the flash.

Is photography allowed in school? I will
look into this.

ON THE TRAIN

Washington, D.C.,
is a great place to take pictures.
Since I'm a photography nut,
you can understand why I was
very excited
for the sixth-grade class trip to D.C.

Of course, I was also excited to be going on a trip for a weekend with my best friends, who are all in my class: Gum, Sam, and Cat. Oh, and I'm Edward G. Garrison, but my friends call me Egg.

My friends and I were sitting together near the back of the train. Gum and I were sitting across from Cat and Sam.

"When does the lunch cart come around?" Gum asked. "I'm starving. I feel like I haven't eaten in days!"

Cat laughed. "I don't think there's going to be a lunch cart," she said. "That's why Mr. Spade told us all to bring a bag lunch."

Gum frowned and flopped back in his seat. "I know, I know. But I was hoping for a little extra something," he said. "Such as dessert."

"Hey, look at this," I said. I leaned forward and opened up the magazine I'd been flipping through: *Cameras and Photography This Week.*

"There's a big sale in Washington, D.C., this week at a place called Washington's Photography," I said, pointing to the full-page ad. "What a lucky coincidence!"

Gum shrugged, and Sam smiled a little. "That's terrific," Cat said nicely. I know my hobby isn't too interesting to my friends, but Cat is always so encouraging anyway.

"Yup," I said. "I've been meaning to get a new tripod! And there are some lenses that seem good."

Just then, Gum's mother pushed through the door from the next car. She was one of the parent chaperones for the trip.

"Hello, kiddies!" she shouted, waving at us. Everyone in the car looked at us.

Gum covered his face. "Oh no," he groaned.

Sam leaned over and tapped his knee. "This might not be as bad as it seems, Gum," she said quietly. "She's carrying a paper sack."

Gum perked up, but still kept his hand over his face. Cat and I looked at each other and shrugged.

By then, Gum's mom was right next to us. "Sit up straight, James," she said, smiling. "Your friends sit so nicely."

I looked across at Sam and Cat. Neither of them seemed to be sitting up very nicely, I thought. But I made an effort to sit up a little straighter.

Gum did too, but I could tell he wasn't happy about it.

Gum's mom messed up his hair. "Thank you," she said. "Now, I'm sure you haven't had your lunch yet, but I wanted to drop off these cakes I made for the train ride."

Gum sat up even straighter as he grabbed the paper bag. "Thanks, Mom," he said. "I was just saying I wanted some dessert."

"Yeah, thanks, Ms. Shoo," Sam said. "What a nice surprise!"

Gum's mom smiled. "That's all right," she said. "You enjoy them . . . after you eat your lunches, please! Some chaperone I'd be if I let the students have dessert before lunch!" She winked at us. Then she waved goodbye and headed back to her own car.

Gum immediately opened the bag and began distributing the treats. There were exactly four amazing-looking coffee cakes. They were covered in those crumbly bits on top that make every bite so good.

Right away, Gum stuffed about half of a cake into his mouth.

Cat's jaw dropped. "Gum!" she said. "Your mom said to wait till after lunch!"

Gum waved her off. "Oh, please," he said. "I ate my lunch while we were on the bus on the way to the train station."

We all laughed. Gum loves his mom's cooking, I guess.

"So, what do you guys think?" Sam said suddenly and quietly, leaning forward. It seemed like Sam wanted the rest of us to lean forward too, so we did.

"What do we think about what?" I asked quietly. "The cakes? They're really good. Gum's mom is a great cook."

Sam punched me lightly on the shoulder. "No, silly," she said. "This trip! What crime do you think we'll solve this time?"

Gum reached into the paper bag, but Cat grabbed his wrist before he could eat another cake. "How about the crime of who ate all the coffee cakes?" Cat said with a smirk.

"Yeah, Gum, those are for sharing," Sam said. She grabbed the bag from Gum. "Now be serious. We'll be pulling into Union Station any minute. We have to be ready."

"Come on, Sam," I said. "We're not superheroes or something. We're just going on a class trip."

"Yeah," Cat added, "it's not like there's always a major crime wave whenever we go on a class trip."

Gum frowned. "Yeah there is," he said.

"Yeah," Sam said. "Name one trip we've been on that didn't involve us busting some crook or scoundrel or vandal or punk?"

Cat and I thought about it, but we couldn't come up with one. They were right. For us, field trips meant fighting crime.

"Okay then," Sam said.
"Then it's agreed: we are
a crime-fighting
team.
Now let's talk about this trip."

CHAPTER TWO

UNION STATION

The train pulled into Union Station right on time. Mr. Spade and the chaperones — Gum's mom and Anton Gutman's mom — led us along the platform toward the big main lobby.

"This station is just over a hundred years old," Mr. Spade called back to us as we walked through the station.

Gum's mom was busy doing a head count. Anton's mom was busy chatting on her cell phone. I don't know who she was talking to, but she sure was loud.

"When it was finished in 1908, it was the biggest train station in the whole world," Mr. Spade continued. "Union Station is the D.C. landmark that has the most visitors every year. Kind of funny that a train station would be so popular."

Sam elbowed me. "It's how everyone gets here," she said. "Of course they visit the train station. How could you not?"

Then we entered the main part of the station. It was huge! There were people everywhere. Pieces of paper were strewn about the floor. And suddenly, everyone was screaming!

A huge group of people ran right toward us, yelling and shouting and looking back over their shoulders. They pushed past us toward the departing trains.

"What was that all about?" Sam said, watching them run off.

Gum pointed into the huge lobby. "Look at that!"

The whole class stopped and looked. Huge crowds of people of all ages and races and shapes and sizes were heading for the exits at full speed. A few people got knocked over. Some people were shrieking. One girl passed out near the newspaper stand.

"What is going on here?" Cat asked. She grabbed Sam's arm and hid behind her. That's easy to do, since Sam is the tallest person in our grade.

A police officer came pushing through our group from behind us. "Stand aside, please," she said. "Don't panic, don't panic."

When she got to the front, she pulled out her walkie-talkie. "This is Officer Parsons. I am in position," she said. "I don't see any ghost."

"Ghost?" Gum whispered to me.

Whoever was on the other side of the walkie-talkie replied, but it was too fuzzy for us to hear.

Then Officer Parsons said,

"Yes, sir. It's crazy here. Some people spotted the ghost of George Washington."

"The ghost of George Washington?" I repeated, shocked. The police officer looked at me and scowled. I quickly turned away and went over to Cat and Sam. Gum followed me.

"Did you guys hear that?" I said. Gum's mother joined us. I noticed Anton was listening too.

"That cop said someone spotted the ghost of George Washington in the train station," I said. Cat's jaw dropped and Sam's eyebrows went up.

Anton Gutman just smirked.

CHAPTER THREE

HAUNTED HOTEL

"Ghosts don't exist," Sam said. "It's a simple fact."

We had already checked into our hotel and were sitting in the hotel restaurant having supper. The real sightseeing wouldn't be until the next day, since it was already pretty late. The train trip had taken most of the day.

"You don't know that," Cat said. "Just because you've never seen a ghost doesn't mean there's no such thing as a real ghost."

Just then, our least favorite person came over to our table: Anton Gutman. He had ketchup on his chin and he was smiling, as usual. But he doesn't have a very nice smile. It's more like the smile of the cat who ate the canary, as the saying goes.

"Hey, you losers," Anton said. "So, you don't believe in ghosts, huh?"

Gum looked at Anton. "Do you need something," Gum asked, "besides a napkin?"

Cat laughed and held up a napkin. Anton grabbed it and quickly wiped his chin. "Did you know that this is one of the oldest hotels in Washington?" he asked.

I shrugged. "Of course," I said. "Mr. Spade told us when he was checking us in. So what?"

"So," Anton said, closing his eyes for a moment, "it's also the hotel with the most ghost sightings in the whole country! And most of the sightings are of President George Washington."

We all stared at him.

"The same ghost that was at the train station," Anton added.

"Go away, Anton," Sam said.

Anton laughed. "Okay, I'll go away," he said. "But I'm telling you, ghosts are real, and this hotel is full of them." Then he walked off.

Sam shook her head, but Cat looked worried.

"Don't worry, Cat," I said, picking up my camera. "He's just trying to scare us. Now smile, okay?"

I held up my camera and Cat smiled. She always smiles for photos.

Gum and I were rooming together, around the corner and down the hall from Cat and Sam. All the chaperones were staying in the rooms between the boys' rooms and the girls' rooms. That meant Gum's mom was just down the hall from us.

Back in the room, I sat down at the desk. Gum popped open a can of orange soda and flipped on the TV. "Let's see what's on TV," he said.

"Okay with me," I said. "I'm going to look at this flyer for that camera store. Maybe I'll get a chance to stop in this weekend and buy a new zoom lens."

"Where'd you get that flyer?" Gum asked, glancing at it.

"They were all over the floor at the train station," I replied.

Gum flipped through the channels until he found an action movie. "Awesome," he said. He fluffed his pillow and then settled back in his bed to watch the movie.

Suddenly, there was a loud crash in the hallway.

Gum sat up. "What was that?" he said.

I strained to listen. There was another crash. Then we heard something being dragged along the carpet outside our door.

Then a low, weird voice yelled, "Never leave for tomorrow that which you can do today!"

Gum and I looked at each other.

The dragging sound got quieter, and then was gone. Gum jumped up and threw the door open. I ran over to look into the hall too.

Just as we put our heads out, a shadowy figure disappeared around the corner.

"Egg," Gum said quickly. "It's a ghost!"

"And," I added, "it's heading right for Cat and Sam's room!"

THE GHOST ATTACKS!

Gum ran back into our room and dove onto the bed. He picked up the phone and dialed Sam and Cat's room.

I stood watching, feeling nervous. "Well?" I said after a moment.

"It's ringing," Gum told me nervously. "No one's answering." He waited a few seconds more, and then hung up.

"That ghost might have gotten them already!" I said. "Think, Gum. What should we do?"

"We have to go save them," Gum said. I nodded, and we were out the door in an instant.

"Wait," I said, turning back. "My camera." I grabbed it off the bureau. Then we were off. Gum and I aren't the most athletic guys in sixth grade, but when our best friends are in trouble, we can move pretty fast.

We tore around the corner and practically slammed into each other when we reached Cat and Sam's door. It was open, but the room was dark inside.

"I can't see anything," Gum said.

There was a crash. The dragging sound started again, on the other side of the room. A voice bellowed, "Our cause is noble. It is the cause of mankind!"

"Hey!" I shouted, raising my camera. "Over here!"

Then I snapped a photo. The flash went off, lighting up the room for a moment. I spotted someone along the far wall and took another picture.

Sam and Cat were huddled under a blanket in the corner behind the bed. The figure was running toward me and Gum.

I snapped another picture. This time the figure almost knocked us down. He had his arms over his face.

I spun around, but he ducked into a stairwell and disappeared. Gum started to chase after him.

Sam got up and switched on a lamp.

"Wait, Gum!" I said.

Gum stopped and looked at us. "We have to catch that guy," he said.

I shook my head. "I have photos," I said. "He's as good as caught."

Sam patted me on the back. "That's our Egg," she said. Cat smiled at me.

"See, Cat?" Sam said. "I told you there was no such thing as ghosts."

Cat looked stunned. "How can you say that?" she said. "We were just trapped by the ghost of George Washington!"

I flipped through my photos until I found the ones I had just taken.

"That wasn't George Washington," Sam said. "Didn't you hear what he said?"

"Here!" I said. "Look at this." I held out my camera for my three friends.

They all said together,
"Anton Gutman!"

CHAPTER FIVE

A BOY CALLED WHAT?

In the morning, Gum and I met Sam and Cat by the elevators to head down to breakfast. When we got to the lobby, though, we forgot all about breakfast.

"I don't know what kind of hotel you're running here," Anton's mom was shouting. "But if you think my son's class is going to stay another minute with a ghost, you've got another think coming!"

"Now, Mrs. Gutman," Mr. Spade said, "please try to calm down."

The four of us made our way over to the desk to listen in. The hotel manager was a young woman and she looked positively terrified of Anton's mom.

Behind the desk, next to the woman, a boy about our age was sitting on a stool. He was watching Anton's mom, too, but he wasn't scared at all. In fact, he was laughing.

He looked at Sam, Cat, Gum, and me. "Can you guys believe this?" the boy said. "They actually think there's a real ghost here."

"Who are you?" Sam asked. I could tell right away that she didn't like him.

"I'm the manager's son," he said. He pointed at the woman who Anton's mom was shouting at. "That's my mom," the kid added.

"Okay, so what makes you so sure it's not a real ghost?" Cat asked.

Anton's mom stopped yelling at the boy's mom. Mr. Spade and Anton's mom came over and listened to us.

Sam turned to Cat. "Cat, I was trying to tell you," she said. "That ghost said one famous thing that George Washington said, but —"

The boy behind the desk cut her off. "But the other thing was a Ben Franklin quote," he said. "It's so obvious."

Sam looked impressed. "Okay, so you figured it out," she said. "But I figured it out first."

The boy shrugged. "Maybe," he said, "but I heard you were hiding under a blanket."

Sam looked at him hard, and for a second, I thought they might have a fistfight. But instead she smiled and put out her hand. "I'm Sam," she said. "This is Egg, Gum, and Cat."

"Interesting names," the boy said. "I'm Crocodile."

Gum and I laughed, and Cat covered her mouth.

"It's a long story," Crocodile said. "Maybe I'll tell you later. For now, call me Crock."

"Okay, Crock," Sam said. "Good to meet you."

Mr. Spade said, "I'm very impressed that you knew enough about our first president and about Ben Franklin to know that ghost was a fake. But even a fake ghost can be a real hassle for the hotel."

"We know who it was," Cat said. She elbowed me. "Show them, Egg."

"Oh, right," I said. I pulled my camera off my neck and switched it on. "See?"

"Anton Gutman," Mr. Spade said, staring at the picture.

Anton's mom clenched her teeth and bit her lip. Her face went red and she looked like she might pop. "Anton!" she shrieked. "Anton Gutman, front and center this instant!"

"Well, I think we should leave this for Anton's mom to handle," Mr. Spade said. He led us away.

Sam turned to wave goodbye to Crock. He waved back.

"Let's get on the bus," Mr. Spade said. "We'll get breakfast on the way to our first stop, the Peace Monument."

THE PEACE MONUMENT

The Peace Monument is in front of the Capitol building in the middle of this huge fountain. It's made out of marble, and is meant to remember the deaths at sea during the American Civil War.

Mr. Spade started reading out of a guidebook. I took some pictures right away. With the Capitol in the background, it was the perfect spot for photos.

Then I spotted a figure moving through the water of the fountain.

"What's that?" I shouted.

Everyone in the class looked, and so did some other tourists.

"It's the ghost of George Washington!" someone shouted. Soon, other people had raised their cameras and were snapping pictures. The ghost, in his full general's outfit, got out of the fountain. It started running toward the Capitol.

"Chase it!" Sam said. She started running after the ghost.

"Sam, wait!" Cat called after her. "It's not safe!"

"That's right," Gum's mother said. "Come back here!"

But Sam didn't stop, and her three best friends couldn't let her run into danger alone.

"Let's go," Gum said. Cat and I nodded, and the three of us followed Sam.

"James!" Gum's mom called. "You come back here right now!" She started running behind us.

Ahead of Sam, the ghost of George Washington turned a corner and was hidden.

We caught up to Sam just before she reached the corner. The four of us rounded the corner together. But the only thing we found was a small parking lot and a man with a camera on a tripod.

"Did you see George Washington come through here?" Sam asked, out of breath.

The man with the camera looked at her like she was crazy. "President George Washington?" he asked.

The four of us nodded.

"Well, no," the man said. "I certainly did not."

"Say," I said, moving closer to the man. "That's a really great camera."

He smiled at me. "Thanks!" he said.

I realized there was a big black case on the sidewalk next to him. "You must have quite a lot of great gear with a case like that," I said.

"I sure do," the man said. "In fact, I own a photo equipment store."

He got up from his stool and took his camera off the tripod. He added, "You know, if you like photography, my store is having a big sale this weekend." He handed me a flyer.

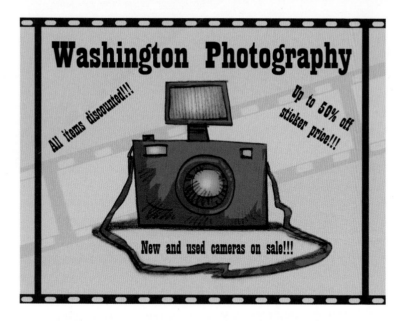

"Oh, I heard about that!" I said. "We're here on a class trip, but I hope I have time to come by."

Just then, Gum's mother came around the corner. She grabbed my collar and Gum's. She couldn't talk, since she was so out of breath. But she looked really mad.

"Hi, Ms. Shoo," Cat said. "We're sorry we ran off."

"Yeah, Mom," Gum said. "Take it easy. We just couldn't let Sam run off alone!"

"Uh-huh," Gum's mom said. "Now let's get back to the group." She dragged me and Gum back around the corner toward the Peace Monument. Cat and Sam followed.

Gum's mom didn't tell Mr. Spade we had run away, so we didn't get into trouble. I mean, besides being chewed out by Gum's mom.

Over lunch, we looked through the pictures I'd taken at the Peace Monument and talked it over.

"I can't understand this," I said. "None of these pictures came out at all. They all look like something was wrong. But I know I took the pictures the right way."

All the photos I'd shot of the ghost of George Washington looked super weird. In every shot, the ghost was way too bright, but everything else in the picture looked normal.

"Maybe it really *is* a ghost," Cat said.

Sam rolled her eyes. "Come on, Cat," she said. "There's no way!"

"I don't know," Gum said. "I think maybe ghosts are real."

"You, too, Gum?" Sam said, looking stunned.

Gum nodded. "When I was little, my family had a small apartment on the east side of town," he said. "It wasn't anything special, but the building had a nice playground."

He leaned forward in his chair. We all leaned in too.

"Well, one night, I woke up and went to get a glass of water in the kitchen," Gum went on. "My mom and dad were already there. They told me to go back to bed, so I went back to my room. But I stood by the door so I could hear what they were saying."

"What were they saying?" Cat asked. She was on the edge of her seat.

"Well, my dad was getting annoyed. I could tell from his voice," Gum replied. "But Mom was scared. And then Dad said, 'Don't be silly. It wasn't a ghost!'"

Cat and I gasped, but Sam chuckled.

"You can bet I didn't get to sleep after that," Gum said. "And then the next day, Mom and Dad sat me down and told me we were moving to a new place across town."

"Because of the ghost?" Cat asked.

"That's what I asked them that day," Gum said. "But they just denied it. They still do!"

"What are you telling these children?" Gum's mom said, standing next to our table.

"Oh, hi, Mom," Gum said.

"You're not spreading that nonsense about a ghost in our old apartment, are you?" Mrs. Shoo asked. "I've told you a hundred times, James. We left because we got a great deal on a place across town, and our landlord was raising the rent!"

"Sure, Mom," Gum said. He flashed Sam a wink.

Gum's mom walked off. "She doesn't want to admit it," Gum said when she was out of earshot, "because she was so scared."

He picked up my camera and pointed to the blur of light where the ghost should have been. "Besides," he said, "everyone knows you can't photograph ghosts. I think it's real. This is our proof."

"Hey, you know what this means?" Sam said. "For once, Gum isn't blaming Anton Gutman for everything!"

CROCK CRIES

After lunch, we all climbed onto the bus to head to the Vietnam Veterans Memorial. The Memorial was built to honor the people who fought in the Vietnam War.

It's a quiet place. The monument itself is a huge wall covered in the names of soldiers.

Very few people were smiling. Lots of people were putting flowers down. Some were making etchings of names with pieces of graphite and tracing paper.

Mr. Spade gathered us around and quietly told us about the memorial. "The designer won a competition to design this monument," Mr. Spade said. "She was only twenty-one at the time."

I felt an elbow in my side. "Ow," I whispered to Sam. "Stop elbowing me."

"Sorry," she whispered back. "But look."

She pointed toward the monument behind Mr. Spade. It was Crock. He was skulking around with his head down. After Mr. Spade's talk, we went over to him.

"Hey, Crock," Sam said.

Crock looked startled. "Oh, hey," he stammered. His face was troubled. "I can't . . . ," he started. "I have to be someplace."

And with that, he turned and ran off.

"What was that all about?"
Cat said.

A moment later, someone shouted, "Look up there!"

We all spun. Above the memorial, the ghost of George Washington had appeared! All around us, people pulled out their cameras and started snapping photos.

I pulled out my camera too, of course. But the moment I raised it to take a shot, someone bumped my arm.

"Hey!" I said.

"Sorry, kid," the man replied. "But I plan to get a photo of that ghost, and I'm not letting some kid get in my way."

He wasn't kidding! In fact, everyone around us was pushing and shoving to try to get a photo of that ghost. It was crazy. I had never seen so many cameras in one place before.

"Let's get out of here," Sam said in my ear. I looked up and realized the ghost had already vanished.

"Okay," I said. The four of us gathered far away from the chaos of photographers.

"It must be Crock," Sam said, shaking her head. "He was acting so weird, and then the ghost showed up. And now both of them are gone. Too bad. I was starting to like him."

"But at the hotel it was Anton," I pointed out.

Sam waved the idea away. "He was just being a dork," she said. "But Crock is up to something. Trust me."

MONUMENT SCARE

Before supper, we made one more stop: the Washington Monument at the other end of the National Mall. That thing is pretty impressive. Mr. Spade said it's over 555 feet tall, making it the highest stone structure in the world.

But when we got to the monument, we barely even noticed it. Instead, we noticed the crowds.

"Is this place always this popular?" Gum asked. "I mean, it's nice and everything. But it's just a big marble pole."

We all laughed.

"Don't you kids know why it's crowded?" a woman next to us said. I looked over and noticed that she was holding a very new — and very expensive — camera. I was instantly very jealous.

A man on the other side of us leaned in. "Everyone wants a photograph of the ghost of George Washington!" he told us.

"That's why it's so crowded?" I asked. "People are trying to see the ghost?"

"He's got to show up here eventually," the woman said. "After all, it's his monument."

I looked around at the crowd. Everyone had a camera, and many of them were brand new. I was pretty jealous of all of them, to be honest.

"I can't believe all these photographers," I said. The four of us tried to push through the crowd. "I've never seen so many cameras!"

"There's a big sale," one of the other tourists told me as we pushed past. "That little store must have had its best day of sales ever. I went down this morning, and it was packed!"

Suddenly a great light flashed in front of the monument. There was a loud howl, and the ghost of George Washington appeared. Cameras started clicking and flashing like crazy.

There was every kind of camera and flash you could imagine. Some were digital, some were film, some were on tripods, some were little handheld cameras. It was a sight to see.

This time, the ghost vanished very quickly. Sam shouted, "Look over there!"

"It's Crock!" Cat said.

"After him!" Gum yelled.

We tried to push through the crowd. But it was hard to move at all, and Crock spotted us. He started pushing through the crowd too, trying to escape.

"We have to reach him before he gets out of the crowd," Sam said, "or he'll easily get away!"

CAUGHT!

Crock didn't have a chance. Sam was at least six inches taller than him, and she's really fast. In just a few moments, she reached over some people and grabbed Crock by the shoulder.

"Stop!" she shouted.

Crock spun to face us. The four of us were shocked to see that he'd been crying.

Sam let go of Crock's shoulder. We had pushed our way through the crowd.

"Are you okay?" Cat asked Crock.

"I'm sorry if I scared you," Sam said.

"You didn't scare me," Crock said. "I'm not crying because of you, trust me."

"Why do we keep seeing you everywhere the ghost is?" Gum asked. Cat hit him on the shoulder. "What?" Gum said. "We have to ask, right?"

"What are you talking about?" Crock said.

"At the Memorial, and the hotel, and now here," Sam said. "We saw the ghost in all those places too."

"Not all of them," Crock said. "The one at the hotel was your friend, remember?"

"Hey!" Gum said. "Anton Gutman is not our friend."

"Fine, fine," Crock said. "Still, it wasn't a ghost."

"Okay," Sam said, "but you were skulking around the Memorial, weren't you?"

"And now you're here at the Monument, too," Gum added.

"I'm only here with my mom," Crock said. "And I go to the Vietnam Memorial every weekend. My grandfather's name is up there. That's why I was crying."

"You miss him?" Cat asked.

Crock shrugged. "I never knew him. But I cry easily, I guess," he said. "That's why everyone calls me Crocodile, like 'crocodile tears.'" He shoved his hands into the pockets of his jeans and stared at his shoes.

Sam asked quietly, "Why is your mom down here today? Shouldn't she be at work?"

"It's her day off," Crock replied. "And she's obsessed with getting a photograph of that dumb ghost, just like every other yahoo in this city, I guess."

Then it hit me. "That's it!" I said, and snapped my fingers. "The pictures! Everyone, follow me."

I took off. I sprinted for the parking lot. I had to hold my camera with one hand to stop it from bouncing against my chest as I ran.

"Where are you running?" Sam said when she caught up with me.

"The parking lot," I replied. "You're faster, go on ahead!" She started running ahead of me. "Look for the man with the camera!" I called after her.

"Got it!" she yelled back.

Sam is very fast. She easily left the four of us in the dust. When we finally caught up, Sam was leaning against a car. The man we'd seen in the parking lot at the Capitol threw a black case onto the passenger seat and went around to the driver's side.

"Is this the guy you mean?" Sam asked, pointing her thumb at the man in the car.

I nodded with a smile. "That's him," I said. "I have a feeling if you open that big black case on the passenger seat, you'll find a George Washington costume — covered in little mirrors, by the way."

"That's an interesting theory, kid," the man said, trying to close the door. Sam didn't budge. "Too bad I'm not about to hand my case over to you."

"Of course you won't,"
I replied.
"Because you know
you'll be busted."

"How do you know this is our ghost, Egg?" Cat asked.

"Don't you see?" I said. "Here are the clues. At the first sighting, I found flyers from his store all over the station floor."

"True," Gum said.

"Then, at the second sighting —" I went on, but Sam interrupted me.

"The second was Anton," she said.

"Right," I agreed. "So at the third sighting, we learned that for some reason photos of the ghost turned out funny. Only a pro photographer like him would know how to prepare a costume to have that effect on the pictures."

"Good point," Sam said, crossing her arms.

"And finally, it hit me," I went on. "Look how well his store is doing thanks to the ghost! It's like the people in the crowd were saying. Everyone wanted to get a photo of this ghost, so they went to his sale — the only big camera sale going on in D.C. right now!"

"That's right," Crock said. "Even my mom bought a new camera just to get a picture of that ghost. And she went to Washington's Photography to get it."

The man glared at Egg. "You're a pretty smart guy, aren't you?" he said. "Well, it doesn't matter, because I don't plan to stick around."

He started his car, even though Sam was leaning on it. Cat shrieked, and that did the trick.

"What's the trouble over here?" a voice shouted. It was a police officer, and he was heading over to us.

"Nuts," the man said.

"Well, Mr. Washington," the cop said. "How's business?"

"Um, great!" the man said. "Best weekend sale ever."

"Tell him why," I said.

The cop glanced at me, and then looked at Mr. Washington again.

"Ask him what's in the case," Gum said.

Sam rolled her eyes. "Officer," she said, "this man has been pretending to be the ghost of President Washington."

"Is that right?" the cop asked. "Why don't we have a look in that case?"

"Okay, I admit it!" Mr. Washington said. He jumped out of the car. "But it's not what you think. It's not what these kids think!"

"Take it easy, Mr. Washington," the cop said. "Why don't you just tell me what's going on."

"I never meant to hurt anyone," Mr. Washington said. "I went up to New York to rent a glittery George Washington costume — I got a great deal — for the big sale. You know, because it's Washington's Photography."

"I see," the cop said.

"But while I was in New York," Mr. Washington went on, "the suit I was wearing got splattered by a bus. I changed into the costume on the bus. I thought it would be funny."

"And when you got to Union Station," the cop said, "people thought you were a ghost?"

Mr. Washington nodded. "I guess I kind of panicked," he said, turning red, "what with all that screaming and running around." He shook his head, and then added, "I even dropped a huge box of flyers I'd had printed up, too, as I ran off. It was not my best day."

"So why continue?" Sam asked. "It was an honest mistake."

Mr. Washington looked down at the ground. "Well, that evening I had so many customers at my store," he said. "Everyone wanted to buy a camera just to photograph this ghost. It was on the news and everything!"

The cop scratched his head. "I'm not sure just what to charge you with," he said. "But I have a feeling we should talk it over with my sergeant."

The cop began leading Mr. Washington away, but then he stopped and looked at us. "And you kids," he said. "That was some serious sleuthing. Who are you, anyway?"

"It was all Egg," Sam said, smiling at me. I felt my face getting hot. "That is, Edward Garrison," she explained.

The cop reached out to shake my hand. "Good job, Egg," he said. "Are you a D.C. native? We could use a man like you on the force."

"No, we're not from here," I replied.

"We're just a crime-fighting team on a field trip."

literary news

MYSTERIOUS WRITER REVEALED!

Steve Brezenoff lives in St. Paul, Minnesota, with his wife, Beth, their son, Sam, and their small, smelly dog, Harry. Besides writing books, he enjoys playing video games, riding his bicycle, and helping middle-school students work on their writing skills. Steve's ideas almost always come to him in his dreams, so he does his best writing in his pajamas.

arts & entertainment

CALIFORNIA ARTIST IS KEY TO SOLVING MYSTERY – POLICE SAY

Early on, C. B. Canga's parents discovered that a piece of paper and some crayons worked wonders in taming the restless dragon. There was no turning back. In 2002 he received his BFA in Illustration from the Academy of Arts University in San Francisco. He works at the Academy of Arts as a drawing instructor. He lives in California with his wife, Robyn, and his three kids.

A Detective's Dictionary

bellowed (BELL-ohd)—yelled loudly

chaperone (SHAP-ur-ohn)—someone who watches over other people

coincidence (koh-IN-si-dunss)—a chance happening

departing (di-PART-ing)—leaving

figure (FIG-yur)—a person's shape

hobby (HOB-ee)—something you enjoy doing in your free time

manager (MAN-uh-jur)—someone in charge of a business

memorial (muh-MOR-ee-uhl)—something built to help others remember something

monument (MON-yuh-muhnt)—a building that is meant to remind people of an event or person

quote (KWOTE)—something someone said

sighting (SITE-ing)—a time something was seen

structure (STRUHK-chur)—something that was built

theory (THIHR-ee)—an idea or opinion

Egg Garrison
6th Grade

Washington, D.C.

Not everyone knows that the very first capital of the United States was Philadelphia, Pennsylvania, not Washington, D.C. But it's true! Washington, D.C. did not become the capital of the U.S.A until 1790.

The capital is named after George Washington, the first President of the United States. The city was planned to be exactly 100 square miles.

There are many important buildings and landmarks in Washington. The U.S. Capitol building construction began in 1793 and was not complete until 1819. Reconstruction projects continue to happen.

The White House, where the President lives, is another important building. Construction began in 1792 and was completed in 1800.

During the War of 1812, Washington, D.C. was invaded and burned by British forces. Many landmarks, including the Treasury, Capitol, and White House, were burned.

One more recent landmark is the Vietnam Veterans Memorial. More than 1,400 people competed in the contest to choose the design of the Memorial. Construction of the Memorial began in March, 1982 and was completed in October, 1982.

Washington, D.C., is always changing. I wonder what monument or memorial will be built next!

Egg: Great job. My favorite thing that we saw in D.C. was the Washington Monument. It reminded me a lot of a pencil. Pencils are cool. –Mr. S

IN YOUR OWN DETECTIVE'S NOTEBOOK . . .

1. At the Vietnam Veterans Memorial, we saw people making etchings. Make your own by following these steps:
   1. Find an object with raised or carved letters. (Try gravestones, store signs, etc.)
   2. Place a piece of paper over the letters.
   3. Use a soft pencil or crayon to gently rub the paper over the letters. You should see outlines of the letters appearing on the paper.

2. If you could go to Washington, D.C., what would you want to see? Write about it.

3. My friends and I solved this mystery. We love solving crimes. What is your favorite thing to do with your friends?

FURTHER INVESTIGATIONS

CASE #FTMOTEDC

1. In this book, my friends and I visited Washington, D.C. In a small group, plan a field trip. Where would you go? What would you do there?

2. Anton Gutman can be really mean. What are some good ways to handle a bully?

3. Have you ever gone somewhere without your parents? How do people behave differently when they're with their parents than when they're not with them?

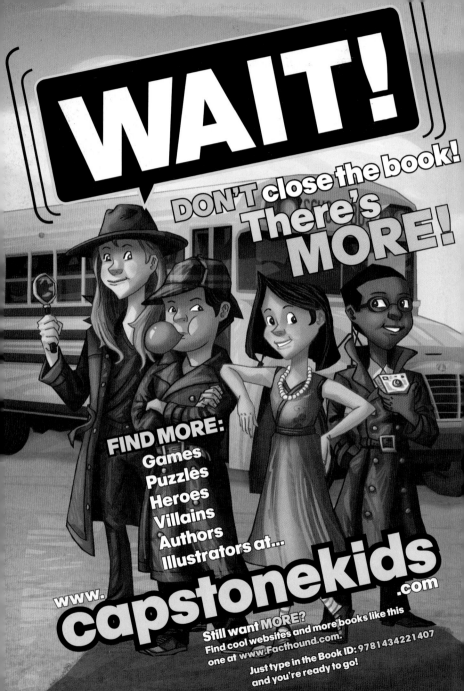